Borzoi Books for Young People

BY

ANNE COLVER

Yankee Doodle Painter
Old Bet
Borrowed Treasure
Secret Castle

PUBLISHED BY
ALFRED A. KNOPF

❦ SECRET CASTLE

Secret Castle

by
ANNE COLVER

Illustrated by **VAIKE LOW**

19  60

ALFRED A. KNOPF : NEW YORK

L. C. Catalog card number: 60–5512
© Anne Colver, 1960

THIS IS A BORZOI BOOK,

PUBLISHED BY ALFRED A. KNOPF, INC.

FIRST EDITION

TO
FLORENCE McDONELL,
Librarian of the Holland Library,

For generously allowing herself to appear as the
only "true" character.
The book is gratefully inscribed.

*The town of Alexandria Bay, N.Y., Devil's Oven Island,
and the fascinating Boldt Castle itself, landmark of the
Thousand Islands, are "true" settings for this imaginary
story.*

❧ SECRET CASTLE

🎝 *One*

🎝 **O**N A warm May evening, just after supper, Molly-O Moore raced across three back yards and a brook from her house to that of her friend, Pip Parker.

"I have the most wonderful news in the world," Molly-O announced breathlessly. "I'll give you three guesses what."

The Parkers had just finished a barbecue supper on their back terrace. Mrs. Parker was in the kitchen, where the electric dishwasher mumbled and splashed to itself, while Mr. Parker played baseball with Jim and Bim, the twins. Pip had been dropping paper napkins into the grill to watch them blister on the hot coals. She looked up quickly at Molly-O's startling announcement.

"Wait a minute—let me think—" Pip ruffled her black bangs and scowled—but not for long. She and Molly-O had been best bosom friends ever since their families had been neighbors in the Ridge, so naturally each one practically always knew what the other was thinking.

"A year ago," Pip began slowly, *of course,* the most wonderful news in the world would have been that you were getting a horse. But since we already have Treasure for our very own, *that* can't be it. Let me think—" Her frown deepened, then she looked up brightly. "I know! You've won a beauty contest and you're going to Hollywood to be a movie star."

Molly shook her head. "Not yet," she said modestly.

"Oh—" Pip looked disappointed, but she tried again. "Well—have they discovered oil digging for the new patio in your back yard?"

Molly gave her head another shake.

Pip hesitated a moment longer before her last guess. "There's only one thing left," she said decidedly. "Your father must have decided to build a swimming pool!"

"Not quite—but you're getting *warm*—because it *has* something to do with swimming. Anyway, I'll tell you—" Molly drew a long breath. "First of all Daddy's office is sending him up to the St. Lawrence Seaway next month—"

"What's the Seaway?" Pip interrupted.

"It's something they've made so ships from across the ocean can come straight up the St. Lawrence River all the way to the Great Lakes, and Daddy says it's very important—but never mind about that *now*—" Molly-O hurried on. "The really important thing is that Daddy is going to take Mommy and me with him to Alexandria Bay in the Thousand Islands—"

"The what?" Pip shook her black bangs, looking baffled.

"Wait until I finish *explaining*." Molly shook her own yellow pigtails in return. "The Thousand Islands are *in* the St. Lawrence River. We're going to stay in a motel cottage right on the edge of the river where we can swim every day and look right across to Canada, Daddy says. But the best part—" Molly-O drew her longest breath for the grand climax, "is that you're invited to come with us—if your mother and father will say *yes*."

It didn't take long for Mr. and Mrs. Parker to agree that Pip could go. From that moment on, the girls planned every detail of the trip. They spent hours, in the swing in Molly-O's side yard, designing imaginary wardrobes, packing and unpacking imaginary suitcases.

6 🏯 SECRET CASTLE

First of all they decided to dress as twins, at least for the car trip, and they agreed to wear red shorts and white T-shirts, with navy cardigans. They even considered dyeing Molly-O's yellow braids to match Pip's black bangs. When their mothers objected, very firmly indeed, Pip sighed. "You never can tell about mothers," she said sadly. "Even the most sensible ones have fits about the queerest things."

On the morning when Pip loaded her duffle and suitcase into the back of the Moore's blue station wagon, she and Molly-O gazed admiringly at each other, especially at their feet in brand-new white sneakers. "Nothing in the whole world looks as clean as new sneakers," Molly-O said, holding out one dazzling toe. "Let's see who can go the longest without getting one single spot on them."

The girls sat on the back seat with a turtle bowl propped carefully between them.

"Mommy wouldn't let me bring half the things I needed," Pip told Molly-O. "She wouldn't even let me put in my rock collection. And she said I was too old to travel with a stuffed panda bear. You know perfectly well Panda has never slept without me."

"Never mind, we've got Edgar and Edna," Molly-O said comfortingly, patting the turtle bowl beside her.

The girls had agreed that a vacation without any pet was unthinkable. Their most important pet, by far, was Treasure, their horse. Then there was Captain Midnight, Molly's cocker spaniel, and Pip's ginger cat. But Mr. Moore had reminded them that people who ran motels did not generally allow pets.

It was hardly likely, the girls admitted, that any motel would allow a horse as a guest. "At least we can write letters to Treasure and put lumps of sugar in them, so he won't forget us," they said.

Not even the fussiest motel owner could object to a pair of turtles, the girls had decided. And it was cozy to have Edgar and Edna between them on the back seat.

Mr. Moore had bought the turtles in New York, Edna for Molly-O and Edgar for Pip. Edgar had the Empire State Building painted on his shell, and Edna had the Statue of Liberty; but after a number of scrubbings, the paintings were getting faint.

"If they ever wear off," Pip said, "we'll never be able to tell them apart."

"I will," Molly said. She leaned fondly over the bowl. "Edna's prettier. I think she's beginning to grow eyelashes."

Since Edgar and Edna lived in the same bowl, the girls had hoped they might decide to get married and have thousands and thousands of children; but so far, they seemed to be satisfied with just being good friends.

By the end of an hour the girls complained that they were starving and Mr. Moore suggested stopping for ice cream cones.

"Chocolate chip for me," Molly-O said happily, getting out of the car.

"Fudge-ripple for me," Pip added.

"Sometimes I wonder why they bother making other kinds of ice cream," Mrs. Moore said.

"I know," Pip nodded. "I used to feel so sorry for the flavors hardly anyone orders. But I never felt sorry enough to give up fudge-ripple."

As they went back to the car, a dribble of chocolate chip landed on Molly-O's shoe. She dabbed at it with a paper napkin. "Well, there's the first spot," she gave a sigh of relief. "Now we don't have to bother about keeping our sneakers clean any more."

The girls spent the next hour reading recipes from a magazine, deciding which ones sounded best. They agreed on a whipped cream loaf and a nut fudge cake which looked quite simple to make. Each one only needed ten ingredients.

Molly-O's father encouraged them. The trip was supposed to be at least partly a vacation for Mrs. Moore, he said, and it would be nice if the girls could help with the work.

"We'll do more than help," Pip said eagerly. "Mommy gave me a whole list of ways to be a good guest. *Don't track in sand or splash up the bathroom, and be sure to hang out wet bathing suits. Remember to say please and thank you. Eat everything on your plate, no matter what and never ar-*

gue. Offer to set the table and always make your own bed . . ."

"Good heavens!" Mrs. Moore laughed, as Pip paused for breath. "With all those rules, we'll feel as though we had Emily Post visiting."

It was late afternoon when they drove under the high-arched sign that said ENTERING THE 1000 ISLANDS, and through the town of Clayton.

The sun had vanished and a pale mist closed in over the road when they came to Alexandria Bay. They found their motel, on the shore of the river.

First, there was the cottage to explore.

"Oh look, what a darling kitchen," the girls said. "And our bedroom window looks right out on the beach. Is it too late to take a swim before supper?" they begged. "Just a little one?"

"A very little one," Mrs. Moore said, "while Daddy and I get unpacked. That is—if you can find your bathing suits quickly."

"Like a flash," Molly-O said triumphantly, as she and Pip dived into their duffle bags. "We packed scientifically. Bathing suits on top—toothbrushes on the bottom!"

The water was warmer than the foggy evening air. The girls raced each other to the float and took turns jumping off the diving board.

Mrs. Moore called them back and they were climbing into fresh clothes for supper and slicking down their wet hair when, suddenly, Molly-O pointed out of the window with her comb. "Look—" she said. The mist had lifted, and out of the river rose the turrets and towers of a castle that seemed to float above the fog. "It's like something out of a fairy story," she said.

Pip hurried to see. "A fairy castle," she breathed. "Only, of course, it can't be real. It must be magic."

Just at that moment a thin shaft of late sun cut through the fog and lighted the towers, turning the windows to gold. Then the mist rose again, and the castle vanished.

"It *is* magic," the girls breathed. "It must be."

There was no time to buy food and cook in the cottage that evening. On their way to a village restaurant for dinner, Molly-O told her mother and father about the castle towers that had seemed to

appear and vanish on the river—like a fairy spell.

"It's probably some old landmark," Mrs. Moore said. "We can ask about it in the town."

"And I want to ask about renting a boat," Mr. Moore said. "If it's a good day Saturday, I'm going to teach these girls to fish."

🕱 *Two*

🕱 **A** FISHING boat to hire?" The slender, blue-eyed woman who brought them their dinner in the *Blue Lantern* restaurant smiled at Mr. Moore. "You couldn't have asked a luckier question." She put down the last plate from her tray—hamburgers and peas, with a double order of french fries for Molly-O and Pip—and reached in her apron pocket. "Here you are—" she handed Mr. Moore a card.

"*Lucky Lady*—" Mr. Moore read aloud. "*For*

Rent to Private Parties. Christie Anderson, Prop.
Finest Fishing on the River."

"And it is the finest, too," the woman nodded proudly. "I'm Mrs. Anderson and Christie is my son. He says he knows every fish in the river by name and sometimes I believe him."

"We'd like to be introduced to a few of his fish friends," Mr. Moore laughed. "Christie sounds like just our man."

"Boy—" Mrs. Anderson corrected him. "Christie's only sixteen, but he's worked as hard as any man since his father died. And kept up his school work too."

"Good for Christie," Mr. Moore nodded. "Could he teach a couple of girls how to fish, do you think?"

Pip and Molly looked up from their french fries. They weren't sure they were going to like fishing, in spite of Mr. Moore's enthusiasm. Pip was worried about having to use worms for bait, and

Molly-O was sure they'd never be able to keep quiet enough.

"Especially since Daddy says we're charter members of the W.G.G.'s," Molly told Mrs. Anderson.

W.G.G., the girls explained, stood for World's Greatest Gigglers.

"Christie will teach you to fish and no giggling about it," Mrs. Anderson promised. "He's showed more than one summer visitor how to bring home a prize catch."

The girls noticed how Mrs. Anderson's eyes glowed when she spoke of her son.

Molly-O had a sudden idea. "If we go out in Christie's boat," she asked, "do you think he'd take us to find the castle on the river? We saw the towers through the fog. They were so dark and mysterious they looked like something magic."

Mrs. Anderson's smile faded. "That's Boldt's Castle," she said shortly. "Plenty of sightseeing launches take tourists to the Island, but I doubt if Christie would take his boat there."

"You mean there *is* a real castle?" Pip demanded eagerly. "We thought we must be imagining things."

"It's real enough," Mrs. Anderson nodded. Her voice still sounded queer and flat. "A man started to build a castle once—years ago. But he never finished." She picked up her tray and started for the kitchen.

"Well, *that's* funny," Pip stared after her in surprise. "Mrs. Anderson sounded almost mad, just because we asked about the castle."

"I don't believe she meant to," Mrs. Moore said. "But it *was* odd. Perhaps she's just tired. She hardly looks strong enough to be handling those heavy trays all day. It's too bad, when she seemed so sweet." Mrs. Moore pushed back her chair. "If you girls are finished, we'll have time to explore a few of the shops before dark."

"Wait till we wrap up a treat for Edgar and Edna," the girls said. They had each saved a crumb of hamburger to fold in paper napkins for the turtles. "After all, they deserve a reward for being such good travelers. And we mustn't forget a lump of sugar to send home to Treasure!"

They had no trouble finding answers to their questions about the castle in the souvenir stores. There were dozens of post cards and posters advertising boat trips to the castle on Heart Island.

"We'll take the trip tomorrow," Mr. Moore promised the girls.

They found just the right card, with a picture of a horse, to send to Treasure, sealed it carefully in an envelope with the sugar lump and addressed it to Mr. Treasure Parker-Moore.

"Now I feel better," Pip said. "Treasure will know we haven't forgotten him. I'm sending a card to Daddy and Mommy too. Then I'm going to get presents for everybody at home. Daddy gave me spending money for the trip, but if I don't buy the presents right away, I'll be sure to use the money for something else."

"I'll help you look," Molly-O said.

They decided on a paper weight for Pip's mother; a tie rack, beautifully painted with *Greetings From The Thousand Islands*, for her father; and a pair of water pistols for her younger twin brothers. "Jim and Bim will simply love them," Pip said. "They can shoot each other from their upper and lower bunks till they're *both* soaking."

Mrs. Moore looked at the pistols doubtfully. "You don't think your mother will mind?"

"Oh, not a bit—" Pip shook her black bangs cheerfully. "Mommy says the only way to bring up twin boys is to give them a room that's like a wrist watch—shatterproof, shockproof and waterproof. Jim and Bim can do *anything* in their room."

Walking back to the cottage, Molly-O sighed. "I

can't wait for morning," she said. "The only trouble with vacations is having to waste time sleeping."

When Mrs. Moore came to tuck the girls in later, she found them at the window, looking out on the river. The mist had lifted and a full moon poured its light on the castle towers. From a tiny rock island nearer the shore, a lighthouse flashed its beam, round and round, across the dark water.

"Maybe there *isn't* anything magic about the castle," Molly-O was saying, "but Mrs. Anderson did say it was deserted and never finished. Any place that's deserted must have some secret, mustn't it?" She turned to her mother.

Mrs. Moore looked at the silvery turrets for a moment. "I wouldn't be surprised," she said slowly. "Every person has secrets. So has every house. I suppose a castle must have its secret, too. But we don't have to guess what it is tonight. Scoot to bed now—" She turned. "Have you brushed your teeth?"

"Practically to a nubbin," Molly-O leaped under the covers.

"And taken your vitamins?"

"Thousands of them," Pip jumped in and pulled the blanket up to her chin. "Isn't it nice to be cool enough to *snuggle?* At home we were practically roasting without even a sheet! Don't forget to kiss Edna and Edgar good-night—"

Mrs. Moore bent obligingly over the turtles' bowl. "Sleep tight." She came over to give each of the girls a kiss. "And pleasant dreams—of castles—"

"With fairy princesses—" Molly yawned into the pillow.

"And secrets—" Pip murmured.

Next morning the sun blazed like warm gold and the sky was blue and clear.

The girls awakened to hear a knocking on their door. "Into your bathing suits," Mr. Moore called. "Swim before breakfast!"

Two minutes later they were fastening their caps. "This is practically rolling out of bed into the water," Molly said happily.

They had hardly reached the raft when Pip turned and pointed. "For heavens' sake, look!" Both girls stared up at the bow of a white ship, looking enormous in the river, and moving so slowly it scarcely made a ripple. The portholes shone in the sun, and rows of people were lined along the rails on the high decks. Some of them were waving and the girls waved back with such enthusiasm they nearly tumbled off the raft.

"It's an ocean liner," Molly explained. "See, it's flying a French flag. Daddy says they made the new Seaway so that big ships from all over the world can come right through this river and into the Great Lakes."

After breakfast Mr. Moore told the girls more about the Seaway.

"First we ought to have a map," he said. "But since we haven't, we'll make our own." Sweeping the dinette table clear, he made a line of knives and forks across the middle. "That's the St. Lawrence River," he said. "Up here is Canada, and on the south is the United States. Over here is the Atlantic Ocean—" He spread out a paper napkin. "Here are Montreal and Quebec—" He broke off two bits of toast, "And here *we* are." He put down a salt-cellar to mark Alexandria Bay.

"I'd rather be the strawberry jam," Molly-O murmured, but her father went on.

"Before the Seaway," he said, "big ships could only come as far in from the ocean as Montreal. Now they can bring their cargoes and passengers right through the Seaway, past us here, and on to Lake Ontario and Lake Erie—" he put down two corn muffins, "all the way to Lake Huron, Lake

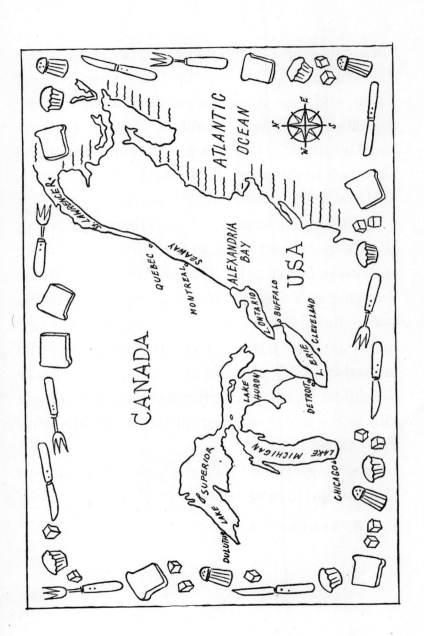

Michigan and Lake Superior—" he made three slices of bread look like the three largest Great Lakes, and then set down lumps of sugar to show the cities: Buffalo, Cleveland, Detroit, Chicago and Duluth. "So you can see how important the Seaway is to shipping," he finished.

"How did they build it?" Pip asked.

"Partly with canals," Mr. Moore answered. "Partly by making locks, so the ships can move up and down, from one level to another; and partly by dredging a deeper channel, the way they did between the shore where we are and your magic castle on the island. That reminds me—" he pushed back his chair, "you're scheduled to take the sightseeing boat trip this morning, including a visit to the castle—so clear off the map while I unlock the car."

Sweeping up the table, the girls popped lumps of sugar into their mouths.

"Pardon me if I eat Chicago and Duluth," Pip said.

"Detroit and Cleveland taste delicious," Molly crunched her teeth. "I just wish they had maps as good as this in school!"

Mr. Moore had to go off on business and could not join them on the sightseeing tour. But before he left, he and the girls stopped at the dock. "I want to be sure we can hire Christie's boat to go fishing on Saturday," Mr. Moore said.

They found *Lucky Lady* at the dock, just as Mrs. Anderson had said they would. Christie, a tall lad with blond, crewcut hair and his mother's blue eyes, was waiting to take out a fishing party for that day. He agreed on a Saturday date with Mr. Moore and the girls.

"Christie's nice—but I don't think he cares much about having girls on his boat," Molly told her mother later. "I'm sure he thinks we'll just fidget and giggle, and spoil the fishing."

"There's not much danger of giggling with Christie," Pip added. "Even when he smiles, he looks awfully serious. Anyway—he says it doesn't matter if we talk in the boat. Fish can't *hear* you, but they can *see* you—especially your shadow. So the important thing is to sit terribly still." She sighed at the prospect. "One good thing," she added more cheerfully, "we don't have to worry about worms. Christie says we use minnows mostly for bait—and they're not half so creepy."

The girls sat together as the sightseeing boat wound its way between green islands that dotted the blue river like emeralds. They squinted in the sunlight while the launch passed island after island after island.

When the sightseeing guide said there were not

really a *thousand islands,* but more than seventeen hundred, Molly and Pip relaxed. "At least we don't have to bother to count them," they said.

The islands were every size, from the smallest, scarcely more than the top of a rock, to Wellesley Island, the biggest, with streets and houses, and even farms, with cows grazing in the pastures.

One island, just large enough for a single house, lay on the boundary line between the United States and Canada. The American flag flew from one door of the house and the Canadian flag from the other.

"What a wonderful place for smugglers to visit," the girls exclaimed. "They could smuggle diamonds and rubies and pearls across the border every time they went from the living room to the kitchen."

The boat made a wide circle and passed back under the high silver span of the bridge between Canada and the United States.

Presently they passed an island with a cave under the rock foundation, and the guide pointed to it. "Devil's Oven," he said, "was the hideout, years ago, of a famous pirate named Bill Johnson. He hid in that cave day and night when he was afraid of being captured."

The girls looked at the dark hole, where the water lapped against the rock sides, and shivered. A moment later, however, they straightened eagerly.

"It won't be long until we come to the castle," they said. Molly peered along the sunlit river. "The guide book says the castle is our last stop on the trip."

Just before they came in sight of the castle's high stone turrets, Pip pointed to a tiny island where a tumble-down little house stood. "The castle isn't the only deserted place on the river," she said. The little house was weathered and gray. Its broken windows stared blankly, with faded blue curtains blowing in the wind, and the front door swung on broken hinges.

"Poor thing," Molly said sympathetically. "It looks so lonesome. I wonder why everybody left it?"

Next moment the girls forgot the forlorn little house as the launch swung toward the castle landing. "Now we come to Heart Island—" the guide's voice boomed through his megaphone. "Spelled H-E-A-R-T because the man who built it, as a gift for his wife, actually changed the shore line of the island to shape it like a *heart*."

The guide went on, telling how the wealthy Mr. Boldt, who had been an owner of the Waldorf-Astoria Hotel in New York, had started to build the castle, more than sixty years ago. He wanted it to be as beautiful as the castles he had seen along the Rhine when he was a boy in Germany. He had built it as a gift for his beloved wife—but when she died suddenly, before it was finished, Mr.

Boldt had ordered work on the castle stopped at the very hour of her death.

Climbing the steep path to the huge front door, Pip paused a moment and gazed up. "How do you suppose such an enormous place could ever have been built for just one family?" She pointed to a smaller building down by the shore. "That was supposed to be the playhouse, the guide said, and it's bigger than both our houses at home put together." U. S. 1108124

When they stepped through the wide front door and actually stood inside the castle, neither of the girls spoke for a moment. Their eyes went from the high ceiling to the huge fireplace framed in wood carving.

"It's beautiful," Molly said softly. Even her whisper echoed in the great empty hall. "I mean —it would have been, if only it had been finished."

They stepped further, walking on tiptoe, and

gazed up through the huge square stairwell, clear to the skylight, far above their heads.

They walked through bare, deserted parlors and the long dining room; then up the grand staircase around the stairwell, to three floors with corridors and corridors of bedrooms.

Once they got lost and came around a corner to meet each other so suddenly they nearly bumped noses. "Gosh—you scared me—" Pip jumped back.

"You did me too," Molly admitted. "This place is *spooky!* The guide said Mr. Boldt built the castle to be big enough for a hundred guests, with all their servants—and I think he was right! Besides that he meant to have a ballroom and a billiard room, and fountains in the garden that would be lighted up at night. Oh, I wish he'd finished it. It would have been just like fairyland."

"My goodness, just think how many people have been here," Pip said. Tourists walked past them in every room. "I just wish we could come

here once without such a crowd," she sighed.
"Maybe then—if the castle has a secret—we could
find it."

On one of the top floors they stepped out on a balcony and looked across the river. "There's Alexandria Bay," Mrs. Moore said. "You can see the hotel—and the restaurant where we had dinner last night."

"And our motel," Pip pointed eagerly. "There's our float."

"And our washing hanging on the line. There are our bathing suits and Pip's red socks," Molly pointed out.

"This must have been an exciting place during the Revolution," Pip said. "With the British troops on the Canadian shore and the Americans right across the river. There could have been a spy right on this island."

"To signal messages back and forth," Molly nodded. "Pip's socks would have meant the Redcoats were arriving on foot!"

Going slowly down the path back to the landing, Pip looked back over her shoulder at the tall stone towers, dark against the sky. "I don't care how many tourists go through the castle," she said. "There's still something lonesome and deserted about it that gives me the shivers."

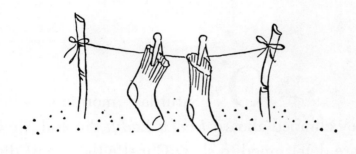

❧ *Three*

❧ **O**N Saturday morning, when they climbed aboard *Lucky Lady*, Pip and Molly were determined to show Christie their most dignified manners. They sat like models of behavior, talking only in low, polite tones, until Christie steered the boat into a cove and anchored.

"This is usually a good place," Christie said. "The fish seem to like to take naps here—and they're apt to wake up hungry!"

Molly-O and Pip had their lines baited, ready

to cast; but after a whole hour of sitting still as statues without one nibble, they were discouraged. "I don't see how your father can stand fishing," Pip grumbled under her breath. "With all the rules—it's worse than basketball. *Don't do this, don't do that, don't move, don't let them see your shadow—*"

"I'll bet the fish have rules, too," Molly yawned. The hot sun and the slap-slap of the waves against the side of the boat made her almost too sleepy to talk. "*Don't swim too near the surface, don't bite anything, never eat bait*—oh golly!—" She woke with a start, as a sudden sharp tug sent her line spinning out. "I must have something huge." She reeled in frantically, and before they knew it, something very large and black flopped into the bottom of the boat.

"Ugh—what *is* it? A sea monster?" Both girls squealed as the creature skidded and slithered at their feet. "It looks like a rubber boot—with *fins!*"

"It's an eel," Christie said, hardly bothering to glance over his shoulder at the girls' excitement.

Mr. Moore was more sympathetic, as he scooped up the wriggling, ugly thing and tossed it over the side. "Too bad," he said, "but that's fisherman's luck. There's nothing to do but toss it back and try again."

The next strike was Pip's. She landed a lively perch. Then Mr. Moore brought in a northern pike and they had one catch after another.

They were almost ready to turn back for shore when Molly had a sudden strike, and her line spun out as something like a streak of silver lightning raced through the water. "Daddy—Christie—somebody come and help," she called frantically.

"You don't need help," her father called back. "Just reel him in. Faster—"

Molly reeled as fast as she could.

"Not *that* fast—" Christie warned. "Take your time—play him out a little—let him run or he'll break the line. *That's* right—easy now—but not *too* easy. Make him know you mean business!"

Molly worked frantically, trying to follow all their directions at once, reeling and tugging at the line. After what seemed like hours, her arms ached and her fingers were numb. "I just can't hold on any longer," she gasped. "He'll *never* give up!"

"Yes he will! Hang on!" they encouraged her. "He's getting tired now—"

"Not half as tired as I am," Molly's hat slipped down over her nose as she made a last desperate effort and a flash of silver broke above the water.

"You've got him!" Christie exclaimed. He handed Pip the net. "Hold fast, now, while we scoop him in—"

A minute later they bent admiringly over the handsome muscalonge. "He's a beauty," Christie said admiringly. "He's small for a muskie, but he must be a good seven pounds. And it's seldom you

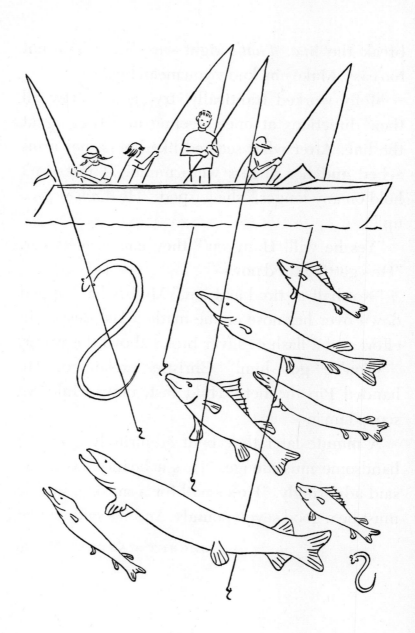

catch one this early in the summer. Too bad you'll have to put him back."

"Put him back?" Molly had been nursing a blistered finger. She straightened up indignantly. "After all the trouble I went to and *he* went to—" she pointed at her fish, "why in the world would I put him back?"

"Because he's a muskie. And the muscalonge season doesn't open until July first—that's next week." Christie paused at Molly's expression of dismay.

"Oh, *no*—" Molly wailed.

"You can't make her put him back when she worked so hard," Pip protested loyally.

But Christie and Mr. Moore were firm. Fishing was a sport, they explained, and part of good sport was obeying rules. "Back he goes," they said.

As Molly-O tossed her beauty over the side, she watched him swim away with a parting sigh. "Just you wait," she shook her finger at the silver flash of the fish's disappearing tail. "I'll be back to get you the *minute* the season opens."

"We take it all back," the girls told Christie as they climbed out at the dock. "Fishing *is* fun. And it's exciting, too."

Christie only nodded. But as he handed the full basket of fish up to Mr. Moore, he looked at it almost wistfully. "You've got a fine dinner there," he said. "If you cook it right."

Something in the boy's voice made Mr. Moore pause. He remembered that Mrs. Anderson worked at the restaurant. So Christie would be going home to a supper alone.

"Why not come and eat with us?" Mr. Moore asked. "We could use an expert cook."

Christie was leaning down, making the boat fast. It surprised the girls when he turned eagerly. "Thanks, I'd like that very much," he said.

·   ·   ·

Half an hour later Christie had a fire blazing in the charcoal grill. While they waited for a bed of coals, Molly and Pip coaxed him to go for a swim, and Mr. Moore offered to lend him bathing shorts. By the time the three of them splashed back from the beach to the grill, Christie's seriousness had quite vanished. He seemed so friendly the girls even brought Edgar and Edna out for him to admire.

By the time the fish was cooked, they were all sniffing hungrily. Christie piled the crisp, brown slices on their plates and Mrs. Moore brought bowls of cole slaw and potato chips.

"M-m-m! this is *good*," Molly said after the first bite.

"Absolutely yummy," Pip answered thickly, through a sweet, buttery mouthful. "And I never thought I *liked* fish!"

"There are fish and fish," Mr. Moore said. "But caught fresh and eaten hungry, nothing in the world tastes better!"

"And cooked by an expert," Mrs. Moore added. "We do thank you, Christie."

When it was time to do the dishes, Christie washed while the girls dried and put away. They took turns telling jokes and riddles. The sillier they were, the funnier they seemed.

Suddenly Christie said, "I've got one! *Why did the sailor's mother knit three socks? Because her son wrote home he had grown another foot since he joined the Navy.*"

Slipping a saucepan into the cupboard, Molly whispered to Pip, "Listen to Christie laugh. He sounds almost like a member of the W.G.G.'s! While he's in such a good mood, maybe we dare ask if he'll take us out to the castle sometime."

The moment they asked him, however, they were sorry. The laughter died out of Christie's face as though a light had been suddenly snapped off. "The castle's only meant for tourists to stare at," he said sharply. "If you want to go, there are plenty of sightseeing boats."

When Christie left a little later, his smile had not come back. His goodbyes were polite enough, but there was no twinkle in his blue eyes as he shook hands stiffly.

"Honestly—" Pip said, as the girls watched him go. "What made him *change* like that? Just when he seemed to be enjoying himself—"

"And you remember," Molly added, with a puzzled frown, "his mother seemed just as queer when we asked *her* about the castle. Oh dear, I wish we hadn't said anything. Now we may never see Christie again."

"Nonsense, of course you will," her father said briskly. "He's taking us fishing again next Saturday and he'll have forgotten the whole thing. You'll see."

Mrs. Moore said nothing. But she watched the boy disappear down the lane with an anxious look on her face.

A few mornings later the girls woke to the sound of a chilly rain that drummed against the windows like streams of lead.

When Mrs. Moore called them to breakfast, they came to the table wrapped in their warmest housecoats, with their icy toes curled snugly in woolen socks borrowed from Mr. Moore's bureau drawer. While they drank hot cocoa and ate scrambled eggs and bacon, they gazed sadly at the streaming window panes.

"We'd planned to take a picnic lunch in the motel rowboat and go exploring along the river," Molly-O told her mother. She took a scalding hot swallow of cocoa and opened her mouth, fanning energetically. " 'Ow ehehing's 'oiled—"

"She's trying to say 'Now everything's spoiled,' "

Pip explained. "Now we'll have to think of something else to do."

Mrs. Moore came back from marketing later and found that Pip and Molly-O had kept themselves busy. They had made their beds, baked two pans of brownies—one not nearly as burned as the other—and given Edgar and Edna a scrubbing in the sink. They had set up a game of *Monopoly* and Molly was already collecting rent on Boardwalk property.

"Finish the game later," Mrs. Moore said. "Let's have a quick lunch and then get into your boots and slickers. The Holland Library is open this afternoon and I'll show you how to go exploring even on the rainiest day. I'm sure you'll find books there that will tell you all the history and stories about your castle you want to know."

Miss McDonell, the librarian, came around from her desk to welcome them sociably. She

showed the girls where to put their wet raincoats and asked what kind of books they liked best to read.

"Any kind as long as they have plenty of horses or ponies in them," they answered promptly. "Or else stories about girls our own age who do exactly the same things we do."

"We've plenty of both," Miss McDonell's blue eyes twinkled. "Those are the books our girls like best, too."

Just today, however, Pip explained, they particularly wanted to read about the castle on Heart Island. "Especially anything that would tell us if there's a mystery about it," she added hopefully.

"I have some reference books on the subject," Miss McDonell nodded. "How much mystery you'll find, I'm not sure, but come and see."

The girls were just turning to follow when someone hurried past them, head down, out of the reading room, and they recognized the familiar figure.

"That was Christie," Molly-O exclaimed. "I wonder what he was doing in the library."

"Christie Anderson?" Miss McDonell looked through the window. "Oh, Christie's here in the library almost every rainy day when he can't take people out in his boat." For a moment Miss Mc-Donell's glance followed the tall lad. "We were all so proud when he won a scholarship to the art school where he wants to study. I've never known a boy who wanted an education more than Christie does—or worked harder to earn the chance." She paused, and then added, "I only hope nothing happens to disappoint him. Sometimes, lately, he's seemed so worried. I've wondered if—" She broke off, and finished more cheerfully. "But then —I expect we all have worries. Now here's our local reference shelf—"

Miss McDonell pointed to a group of books. "You'll find everything we know about the castle there," she said, "and if you like mystery and excitement, here's a story about the pirate, Bill Johnson. He hid in the cave on Devil's Oven Island, and had a pretty daughter Kate, about your age, to row out in the dead of night and bring him food."

"Did she honestly?" Molly breathed.

"I don't know how *honestly*," the twinkle in Miss McDonell's blue eyes deepened. "But that's what the story says. I'm not sure how pleased people were in those days to have a cutthroat for a neighbor, but nowadays we're so proud of having a real live pirate in our history that we celebrate 'Bill Johnson Day' every year. Everyone dresses up with gold earrings and pirate costumes."

For the next hour Molly and Pip turned page after page. They were lost in the fascinating story of how Mr. Boldt had bought the island for his castle more than sixty years ago. How he had started out to build a summer home for his wife and children that would be as beautiful as any of the famous castles on the Rhine he remembered seeing as a boy in Germany. They read how he had sent for workmen and artisans from all over the world—and then, on a day when the castle was still unfinished, how his wife had suddenly died, and Mr. Boldt had ordered all work stopped, and the castle abandoned.

"It's the most romantic story I ever read," Molly-O said when the girls went back to Miss McDonell's desk.

"I wish we knew much more about it," Pip sighed. "I mean, how it all really happened. And how everybody *felt*."

Miss McDonell hesitated for a moment. "If you'd really like to hear more of the story," she suggested, "you could talk to old Dan Tobert. He lives in the stucco house at the end of the street, and everyone calls him 'Uncle Toby.' He worked on the castle himself, and I'm sure he'd tell you all he remembers. In fact—" Miss McDonell smiled, "Uncle Toby is glad to find anyone nowadays who'll listen to his stories."

"You mean—" the girls asked, "he really worked on *building* the castle? And he was there when they stopped working?"

"The very moment," Miss McDonell assured them.

The girls thanked her warmly. Before they left, they filled out library cards and each borrowed a book about a horse. "It's just to make sure we don't forget our own horse, Treasure," they explained.

Miss McDonell nodded understandingly. "You won't miss Uncle Toby's house," she called after them. "It's the one with morning glories on the front porch."

They found Uncle Toby in a small parlor, so crowded with pots of ferns and African violet plants that there hardly seemed to be enough room left for the furniture.

Molly and Pip squeezed themselves onto a narrow plush settee, with ferns tickling the backs of

their necks, while Uncle Toby sat down facing them.

"Now, this is a nice surprise on a rainy afternoon," Uncle Toby began cordially. He picked up a big, gray cat and rubbed her ears comfortably as she settled on his knee. "It seems as if Mother must have had a notion we were going to have company, or she'd never have set out to bake ginger cookies."

The girls sniffed the warm, spicy smell that drifted in from the kitchen. It made them pleasantly hungry while they asked if Uncle Toby would be willing to tell them about the building of the castle.

The old man seemed pleased enough to tell them all he remembered. "Bless my soul," he said, "there aren't very many who want to listen to my stories any more. Except Clementina here—" he stroked the cat who purred like a gentle furnace. "Clementina started out a good many years ago as *Clem*," he explained, "but after the first set of kittens, Mother and I thought we'd best change her name. Clementina's given us kittens twice a year ever since, and we found a home for every kitten, but I reckon Clementina's about run down now. She feels she's got a right to a little rest, same as us other older ones."

He leaned back and rocked for a moment. "So you want to know about the time when we worked on the castle—" Uncle Toby's eyes shone. "I can tell you about it all right. I was a carpenter in those days, and I was right out there on Heart Island from the minute they drove the first nail until the telegram came from Mr. Boldt that his wife had died, and we were to stop work and leave the island."

"What was it like when the message came?" Molly-O asked. She and Pip were leaning forward eagerly. "Did everybody feel sorry?"

Uncle Toby shook his head. "Sorry is hardly the word." He frowned, looking out of the window at the streaming rain. "We felt—I guess all of us felt—well, sort of broken off. As if something in our lives wouldn't ever get finished. You know—"

he went on slowly, "it wasn't just a *house* Mr. Boldt was building, or even just a castle. He was trying to make something for his wife that would be the most beautiful place in the world—and he brought people from all over the world to help make it. Some to make carvings and some to do plastering and paneling—they were real artists, some of them. Why, even the children's playhouse down by the pool was going to be grand enough for a prince to live in. There wasn't any trouble Mr. Boldt wouldn't take to make everything perfect—"

The old man paused, still looking out of the window. For a moment there wasn't a sound in the room except Clementina's purring. Then Uncle Toby went on. "The day the telegram came, I can remember how a man went around from one room to another reading the message. We were to stop our work right where we were and leave the island. I can even remember the nail I was pounding in a corner of the dining room floor. I just went off and left it there—half-driven. All around, the workers laid down their tools. It was like something dying—" Uncle Toby sighed. "All that busy sound of hammering and pounding and sawing and plastering and carving had been going on days and months—almost two years. Then, little by little, it just stopped—'till finally there wasn't anything to hear except the men's footsteps walking out and down to the landing for the last time. Nobody talked. We just stood on the dock and waited for boats to take us back to the mainland. I reckon there wasn't a man who left the island that day without looking back and wondering what the castle would have looked like, if we could have finished it the way it was meant to be."

"It sounds just awful," Molly-O burst out. "If I'd been there, I'd've *cried*."

"Where did all the workmen go?" Pip asked. "I mean, those who didn't live around here?"

"Mostly back to wherever they came from, I guess," Uncle Toby said. "Some of the stone masons had come from Italy. I remember one named Tony who used to sing all the time. He sounded just like opera. Then there was Micky—he was a plasterer, who'd come from Ireland. And there was one young fellow we all called Frenchy—because he spoke with kind of an accent. He was a woodcarver and Mr. Boldt had brought him clear from Switzerland, just to carve panels for the castle. Frenchy could take a piece of wood and carve it so fine it looked like lace. He never talked much, but he had the bluest eyes I ever saw. When he'd finish a carving and it was je-e-st right—his eyes would light as if the sun were in 'em." Uncle Toby sighed. "I always thought Frenchy might be a famous artist some day."

"What was his name?" Molly-O asked. "His real one, I mean. Besides Frenchy?"

"I don't know as I ever knew," Uncle Toby

smiled, but his eyes still had a faraway look. "I never heard of him again from that day to this. But I've never forgotten him either."

Mrs. Tobert's gingerbread squares were as delicious as they had smelled. The girls each ate four and drank three glasses of sweet cider apiece.

"Just enough to keep body and soul together until dinner time," Uncle Toby said hospitably, passing the plate of ginger squares again while he told them more stories of the castle.

"When my own boys were young," he said, "they loved the castle. In the summer time, they'd row their boats out and climb all over the place. And in the winter, when it was so cold the river was frozen over, the boys would walk out to the island across the ice, and play hide-and-seek through those deserted castle rooms till it was long after dark and they'd scared themselves so they hardly dared walk back home."

. . .

When the girls left, Mrs. Tobert shook hands with them at the door.

"I wish my mother could see your African violets," Molly-O said. "She grows them too. Only not nearly as many kinds as you have." Molly looked at the blossoming rows of pink and purple and white that filled the tiny, tidy room.

"I just hope she'll come and call," Mrs. Tobert said warmly. "I do love to meet a new violet friend. You girls come again, too. It does us worlds of good to see young people again. And Papa loves to have someone listen to his stories."

The sky was clearing as Molly-O and Pip turned down the road toward the cottage, and the faintest trace of a rainbow arched across the river. The girls looked in silence for a minute. Each of them was remembering the old man's story.

"Do you suppose—" Pip said wonderingly, "that Frenchy ever did get to be a famous artist?

Of course, he'd be pretty old by now. He might even be dead. But sometimes artists don't get famous until after they're dead—and then all their paintings are terribly valuable."

"We'll never know," Molly gazed solemnly at the dark turrets under the rainbow cloud. She sighed. "I guess whatever happened to Frenchy will always be one of the castle's secrets."

❧ *Four*

❧ LUCKY LADY was waiting at the dock the next Saturday.

Just as Mr. Moore had expected, Christie seemed to have forgotten all about being angry. He helped the girls put their tackle aboard and turned to Mr. Moore. "I hope you're set for some excitement," Christie glanced at the faintly overcast sky and the river smooth as gray glass. "This is just the kind of day fish like to take it easy and catch up on their sleep."

For the first part of the morning they tried trolling their lines from the stern of the boat while Christie idled the engine gently, just enough to keep them moving. He followed the shore line skillfully, gliding past pools and shallows where the fish rested. "It seems almost a shame to disturb them," Molly-O said.

Before noon they had each had several strikes, and Pip had won a tussle with a particularly scrappy bass. "Whew—that was something—" she mopped her forehead on her sleeve when the flopping, thrashing fellow was finally landed. "I thought I had a whale that time—with Jonah inside him!"

Mr. Moore laughed. "No rubber boots with fins today," he said. "And not a single squeal all morning. You know, Christie, I really believe we'll make fishermen out of these girls yet."

"We've been using the motel rowboat and practicing during the week," Pip admitted. "It's too long to wait between Saturdays now that we've discovered fishing is fun."

Christie grinned approvingly, but his eye was on the horizon where a low bank of clouds was piling up. "I hate to spoil a run of good luck," he said, "but I don't like that sky."

"Oh, please—wait till we have one more chance," the girls begged.

At the first growl of thunder, Christie delayed no longer. He swung hard about and headed *Lucky Lady* for home. It was too late. Even at her fastest, she was barely in sight of the bay when the storm broke. Lightning zigzagged over their heads and thunderclaps exploded. The river was whipped into whitecaps that slapped the side of the boat and sent the spray flying. Just as they rounded the point toward the dock, a heavy, pelting rain came down.

"I'm getting soaked," Molly gasped.

"Me too—" Pip pulled a sweater around her shoulders miserably. "I saw Christie put some slickers in the forward compartment," she said. "Let's get them."

Wet floorboards and the sharp pitching of the boat made their footing uncertain as the girls struggled to the hatch. Christie and Mr. Moore were too busy at the wheel to notice the girls— but, just as they reached for the slickers, a sudden command from Christie made them jump back.

"Shut that door—"

Even above the noise of the storm, Christie's voice cracked like a shot.

Both girls whirled in astonishment. "We—we only wanted to borrow the raincoats—" Molly began. Her teeth chattered in the damp cold.

Christie didn't answer. He turned from the wheel just long enough to reach past them and push a square box, tied with blue string, back into the compartment. Then he pulled out the slickers and handed them over.

"Those are my things," Christie said angrily. "When you want something on this boat, ask for it."

As the girls huddled under the raincoats, too astonished to speak, Christie swung back to the wheel. Ducking his head against the wind and rain, he managed to bring *Lucky Lady* safely to the dock and they climbed ashore, shivering.

Christie mumbled a goodbye to Mr. Moore, but he was careful not to look at the girls, and two angry spots of color still showed in his cheeks. "You can keep the slickers until next time," was all he said.

No one had breath to speak above the noise of the storm until they reached the cottage, but once inside the door, Molly flung down the raincoat and shook her wet pigtails. "Honestly—" she burst out, "Christie didn't have any right to fly at us like that!"

"Just because we tried to get a couple of raincoats out of the hatch," Pip joined in indignantly. "You'd think he had diamonds or something in there." She flung the dripping black bangs out of her eyes. "And when we had such a good catch.

Sometimes I think Christie doesn't *want* anyone to have fun."

"Now wait a minute," Mr. Moore said. "I'll admit Christie was short-tempered—but remember, he was responsible for bringing us—and his boat —through a bad storm. Let's try to be reasonable about it."

The girls were in no mood to be reasonable. "If Christie Anderson is mad this time, he can *stay* mad," they declared. "We'll never speak to him again."

But when they came to the dinner table they found Mrs. Moore looking so serious that they stopped their grumbling.

"Just listen to me before you say another single word about Christie," Mrs. Moore ordered.

The girls listened, more amazed each moment, while she told the story she had heard that afternoon.

First of all, Mrs. Moore began, she had gone to
the *Blue Lantern* for lunch. When she asked for
Mrs. Anderson, and learned that Christie's
mother was ill, she had decided to go and see her.
"I only meant to take some flowers and visit a few
minutes," Mrs. Moore said, "but I stayed all afternoon. Poor soul, she was desperate for someone

to talk to. I never felt sorrier for anyone in my life—" she shook her head.

It seemed, Mrs. Moore went on, that Christie's mother had been ill several times the winter before. She had some sort of a virus, the doctors said. "They kept telling her she'd have to stop working and take a long rest before she could get really well. But Mrs. Anderson wouldn't give in. She was determined to work, to give Christie the education he wants so much. You know he's even won a scholarship—"

Molly-O nodded. "Miss McDonell told us," she said.

"But now Mrs. Anderson is ill again," her mother sighed. "This time the doctor says she simply can't work again for six months—perhaps even a year—until she's well. She's heartbroken —for it means Christie will have to stay home and take care of her—so he can't take his scholarship."

The girls were silent for a moment. "If his

mother got well—couldn't he take the scholarship next year?" Pip asked.

"I'm afraid not," Mrs. Moore said. "If Christie gives up the chance this fall, he'll lose it forever. It's such a pity—when he and his mother have both worked so hard."

"I'm sorry I ever got mad at Christie—" Pip blinked hard, cutting a slice of applesauce cake.

Molly nodded soberly. "If there were anything in the whole world I could do to help Christie go on to school—I'd do it," she declared.

Mrs. Moore went on to tell them why Christie and his mother had come to Alexandria Bay from California. It was because Christie had been sure there was something hidden in the castle that belonged to them. Something valuable.

"Hidden in the *castle?*" Molly's eyes were round.

"Oh, I knew it—" Pip bounced in her chair. "I knew there was some secret—"

"Only there *wasn't*," Mrs. Moore shook her head. "That's the sad part. Let me tell you how it happened."

While they hung on every word, she told how Christie had lived with his mother and grandmother in California. When Christie was fourteen, his grandmother had died. Going through her desk, they had found a queer-looking note scribbled on an old piece of paper.

"Mrs. Anderson showed it to me," Mrs. Moore said. "There were only a few scribbled words that said: '*Everything left in Chateau . . . Tell sister . . . good-bye . . .*'"

"*Chateau!*" Molly exclaimed. "What does that mean?"

"It means castle in French," her mother said. "But just a minute—" Mrs. Moore put up her hand. "Let me finish."

The girls listened breathlessly as she told them how Christie had grown more and more curious about the mysterious note. He wanted to know everything his mother could remember about its history. When she told him that years ago her mother's only brother had been killed in a train wreck, and that when his things were sent home, the note was with them, Christie was more excited than ever. He was absolutely sure it meant that his great-uncle had left some valuables—perhaps even a fortune—hidden somewhere in a castle.

"Mrs. Anderson said Christie finally found some letters to his grandmother that showed her brother had come from Switzerland to work on the castle at Alexandria Bay," Mrs. Moore went on. "As soon as Christie heard that, he was so determined to get back and search the castle that he persuaded his mother to leave their home and spend all her savings to come here from California."

"And did they find it?" the girls demanded.

Mrs. Moore shook her head again. "All they found," she shrugged, "was that the castle had been open to tourists for years. There wasn't a chance that any treasure could still be hidden, with thousands of people going through the castle. When Christie realized there was no hope of finding anything his great-uncle might have left, his mother said the boy was so dreadfully disappointed he would never speak of the castle again, or ever go near it. And Mrs. Anderson feels almost as bitterly herself."

The girls exchanged a look. "No wonder they both seemed so queer when we mentioned the castle," they said.

"You can't blame them," Mrs. Moore said. "To think of giving up their home and coming all the way across the country—and then to have to give up all their hopes."

"Well, *I* haven't given up—" Molly tossed her head.

"Neither have I," Pip ruffled her bangs fiercely. "When Christie's great-uncle wrote that note, he must have meant *something.*"

"But how can we ever find out what?—" Molly straightened as an idea struck her. "Unless—" she said, "Uncle Toby would know something." She turned to her mother. "Did you say Christie's great-uncle came from Switzerland?"

"And he carved wood?" Pip added excitedly. "If he had blue eyes—like Christie's—"

The girls stared at each other for an electric moment.

"It could be—" Molly-O said.

"It *must* be—" Pip nodded solemnly.

"Christie's great-uncle must have been *Frenchy,*" they said together.

.   .   .

Before they went to bed Molly and Pip decided to visit Uncle Toby the next day. "He might even know where Frenchy would have hidden something," they agreed. "Then we can find it."

"And be the greatest detectives of the century," Mrs. Moore finished with a laugh, as she turned out the light, "but *not* until tomorrow. Right now it's way past bedtime."

When the door was shut, Pip gave her pillow a furious thump. "Sometimes I get discouraged with all grownups," she said, "even ones as nice as your mother. They never think of anything but bedtime."

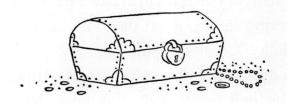

❧ *Five*

❧ **N**EXT morning the girls raced
through breakfast and made a dash for the house
with morning glories on the porch.

Uncle Toby opened the front door with Clementina hanging over his arm like a fur piece. "Good
day, young ladies, good day," he beamed at Pip
and Molly. "Come right in."

The girls hurried to tell him, interrupting each
other in their excitement, the whole story of the
mysterious note that Christie's great-uncle had
left. When they had finished, they looked at Uncle

Toby hopefully. "*Do* you think Christie's uncle could have been Frenchy?" they asked. "And *don't* you think the note meant that he must have left something valuable hidden in the castle? Something that would belong to Christie and his mother now?"

Uncle Toby took a long time to answer. Finally he said slowly, as though he hated to speak the words, "Yes, I'd think it likely that Frenchy was the boy's uncle, all right. But—" there was another pause, while the old man stroked the cat and the girls had to bite their lips and sit on their hands to keep from bursting with impatience.

"But I'm afraid—" Uncle Toby went on at last, "that what Frenchy left behind in the castle was found years and years ago."

"You mean he did leave something?" the girls leaned forward eagerly. "And you actually remember about it?"

"He did," Uncle Toby nodded. "And I do. Quite

distinctly, in fact. I recall that not long after we stopped working and Frenchy had left here, someone found all his tools, right where he'd left them in the castle and—"

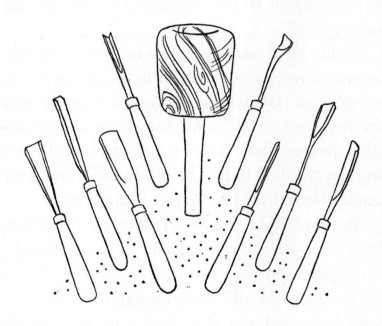

"His *tools*—" Molly broke in with a gasp of dismay. "Is *that* all Frenchy left? I mean—" she and

Pip exchanged a despairing glance, "we thought surely Frenchy's note was talking about something more *important*—"

"Tools are important to a workman," Uncle Toby said gently. "Especially to a woodcarver like Frenchy. Some of his friends gathered them up, I remember, and took them back to the house where he'd lived. It was only a tumble-down bit of a place, on one of the smallest islands, but Frenchy had fixed himself a home there. I expect he meant to come back—and he'd have found his tools waiting for him. But he didn't live to, poor fellow—" Uncle Toby sighed. "No one else ever bothered with the little house. It's stood empty ever since—falling to more rack and ruin every year."

Pip sat up straight. "I'll bet I know exactly the place you mean," she exclaimed, "with the windows broken and faded blue curtains flopping out—"

"We passed it on the sightseeing boat," Molly chimed in.

"That's the very one," Uncle Toby nodded.

Not even finding that they had seen Frenchy's house kept the girls from being bitterly disappointed, however. Uncle Toby's news that Frenchy had left only his tools behind him in the castle was a sad blow. Perhaps, as Uncle Toby said, the tools were important to a *woodcarver*. But how could they possibly be valuable enough to help Christie?

The fresh doughnuts and lemonade that Mrs. Tobert brought out cheered them slightly, but they walked home in gloomy silence, scuffing their sneakers in the dust.

"I feel just terrible," Molly said finally. "I'd hoped so much we could help Christie. But I suppose Uncle Toby's right. All Frenchy left were his tools, and there's just no use hoping."

.   .   .

The rest of the week was bright and sunny.

The girls forgot their troubles and borrowed the motel rowboat to go fishing and exploring.

One afternoon they rowed across the International Boundary line. "Just think, we're in Canada this very minute," Pip said. "If we were smuggling something across the border, where would we hide it? In the heels of our shoes?"

"How could we when we're barefoot?" Molly demanded. "I read a story about smugglers who put diamonds in their false teeth. Of course, that wouldn't help if you didn't *have* false teeth—"

"Or any diamonds either," Pip laughed. "I suppose you'd have to talk this way, with your mouth shut, 'M-mh-mh-mh—'."

On the way home they passed Devil's Oven.

Pip peered into the dark cave in the rock where the pirate had hidden. "I'm glad I'm not Bill Johnson," she shivered.

"I dare you to go in," Molly whispered. "Just a little way—"

"I dare *you*," Pip whispered back. She swung the boat around, and they glided into a black and silent world of rock ceilings and damp rock walls. The water underneath was still and deep.

"My gosh—!" Molly breathed.

Her voice echoed hollowly from the cavern walls and both girls shivered at the ghostly sound.

"I think we better get out of here—" Pip swung the boat around sharply and rowed as hard as she could. "*Whew—*" she mopped her forehead with relief as they floated back into the bright, hot sunshine. "That was awful. Imagine even a pirate hiding in there for days and days."

"And imagine his daughter Kate rowing out to bring him food *in the middle of the night,* the way the story we read in the library said!"

"Thank heavens our fathers aren't pirates *or* smugglers," the girls agreed, and headed for shore.

By the end of another week, however, something had made Pip and Molly realize that smuggling might not be a subject to joke about.

It happened late one night, when Molly woke

up to hear the Venetian blinds rattling against the turtles' bowl on the window sill. She got up sleepily to move Edgar and Edna, but the next moment she was wide awake, staring through the window and calling Pip to come quickly. "Look," she said, pointing, "there's Christie just bringing *Lucky Lady* toward the dock." They could even see the name on the boat's bow in the bright moonlight. *"And he's coming from Frenchy's old house on the island!"*

"What on earth would he be doing out there as late as this?" Pip demanded in amazement. "You don't suppose—" she hesitated, "he needs money so badly for his scholarship that he might be—?"

"*Smuggling*—?" Molly finished, in a whisper.

Pip nodded. "Christie might be leaving something on the island for another boat to pick up and take across the border to Canada."

"Oh, no! I just don't believe it," Molly protested.

"But if it *were* true, what would we do? Tell Daddy?"

Pip shook her bangs decidedly. Her best detective spirit was up. "Of course not! We'll have to investigate. The first thing in the morning we'll take the rowboat out to Frenchy's cabin—and see what we find!"

❦ *Six*

❦ NEXT morning the girls were up early. They watched the dock from their window, and the moment they saw *Lucky Lady* start out with a fishing party they knew Christie was safely out of the way for the day.

They swallowed their breakfasts and made their beds, smoothing over lumps and bumps in the blankets as quickly as possible.

Then they flew for the rowboat at the motel dock.

"It's lucky your mother didn't ask us where we

were going," Pip said, as she fitted the oarlocks. "Goodness knows, we've been out in the boat alone often enough—and I don't *think* she'd mind our going out to the cabin. But sometimes grown-ups pick the most inconvenient times to take one of their notions. I'll row out and you row back. OK?"

Molly nodded. She sat in the stern, watching the little house on the island draw nearer with each steady tug on the oars. "Another thing that's lucky is that we've learned to row," she said. "Remember when we first tried, and the boat kept going round and round in circles instead of forward?"

They found a rickety landing on the deserted little island, and tied the boat to a half-rotted post. Then they picked their way silently up the loose, broken steps and along a weed-choked path to the sagging front porch.

Molly-O hesitated outside the door. "I guess

we just go in," she said, "although it doesn't seem very polite not to knock."

"For goodness sakes, who'd answer except ghosts?" Pip demanded, and stepped inside. As the floor creaked under her foot, she jumped back. "It *is* a little scary," she admitted. But a moment later she went on in her best detective voice, "Well, we might as well begin searching. You start with that room—" she pointed, "and I'll search this one."

Molly-O would have much preferred to have them stay together. Besides, she wasn't exactly sure what to search *for*. But she nodded, swallowing bravely, as she tiptoed through the doorway.

"I just wish I'd brought my fingerprinting kit," Pip called after her. "I'll never travel without it again!"

At the end of an hour both girls were discouraged.

They hadn't found any ghosts, but they hadn't

found any clues either. "I just don't believe Chris-tie could have hidden anything here," Pip said as she wiped a cobweb off her cheek. "I've hunted in every nook and cranny. We've done everything but pry up the floor boards—and there's nothing here—except things that must have belonged to Frenchy." She looked around at the shabby chairs and tables.

"One thing is sure," Molly nodded, "Frenchy must have expected to come back. Or he'd never have left his furniture. And clothes—" she pointed to the closet where garments hung in a dusty row. "Even his kitchen pots and pans—"

"And his paintings—" Pip glanced at a stack of canvases in the corner. "That's an awfully pretty one on top—" She went over to look at a painting that showed a river cove with sunlight coming through the trees in patches like bright copper pennies on the cool, blue-green water. "You re-member, Uncle Toby said he thought Frenchy might be a great artist some day. If he were, I suppose his paintings might be worth a lot of money. But how would anyone know?" she frowned. "We don't even know what Frenchy's real name was!"

"The only thing he didn't leave were his books," Pip pointed to a row of empty shelves beside the desk. "Now, I wonder what he did with those? If he just went traveling, he wouldn't take *books* along—" she broke off sharply as a sudden breeze sent a loose shutter banging.

"Oh my heavens—" Molly looked out of the window toward the landing and gave a quick gasp. "There goes our boat! The wind's changed, and that rotten post we tied it to must have broken. Hurry—" she dashed for the door. "We'll have to try and catch it—"

Pip turned to follow. As she dashed across the room her sneaker caught in the ragged carpet and sent her sprawling. As she scrambled to her feet, she looked down and saw that a corner of the carpet had been pulled loose from the rusty tacks that fastened it. And on the dusty floor, under the flap of faded carpet, Pip saw the corner of a yellowed square of paper.

She leaned down and picked it up. There was only time to stuff it in her pocket as she raced after Molly toward the landing.

"What'll we do if the boat's *gone?*" Molly wailed over her shoulder. "Nobody knows where we are! We're liable to *die* on this island—or at least starve to death."

"Miss McDonell says this used to be called Whortleberry Island," Pip panted, close behind, "I guess we could eat those, whatever they are—"

The next minute Molly shouted back with relief. "Oh, thank goodness—there's the boat!"

Loosened by the wind, the rowboat had blown around a rocky point and nudged into a cove. The girls waded through the shallow water and climbed in, with sighs of thankfulness. "At least

we'll get home without their sending the F.B.I. to find us," Pip said.

Not until they had made fast at the motel dock, did Pip remember the bit of yellow paper she had stuffed in her pocket. She pulled it out and stared at an old envelope for a moment. Then she grabbed Molly's arm. "Look what this says—" she pointed to the envelope with a shaking finger. "It's addressed to *M. Jacques Touraine. That must have been Frenchy's name!* And the stamp says *Helvetia*—that must mean it's from Switzerland! I know because Jim and Bim have Swiss stamps in their collection and they say *Helvetia*. Now if we could just find out if Jacques Touraine is a famous artist—"

"Miss McDonell could help us," Molly-O cut in quickly. "We can look in the library—and if Jacques Touraine really *was* a famous artist, we can find his name there."

"Only the library closes from twelve to one for lunch," Pip said, "and it's almost noon. Let's *run—*"

They reached the library door just as Miss McDonell was locking it. When she saw the girls' anxious faces, she told them to come in.

"My goodness," Miss McDonell said, "you two look as though you'd found a ghost!"

"Maybe we have!" They poured out their story. "We've got to find out whether Jacques Touraine ever *was* a famous artist," they said. "If he was, his paintings will be valuable, and they'll help Christie."

"Then come and see," Miss McDonell said.

When they had checked every reference book on the art shelf, however, there was no Jacques Touraine to be found.

"I'm afraid he isn't in any index," Miss McDonell frowned, "and yet the name sounds familiar somehow," she paused, still frowning.

Molly and Pip told of finding the stack of paintings in the deserted cabin. "We thought if Frenchy *had* gotten famous, like Uncle Toby thought, the paintings might be worth enough to help Christie get his scholarship," they explained.

"Bless your hearts," Miss McDonell shook her head, "those paintings weren't left by Christie's great-uncle Frenchy! Christie painted them himself!" She paused. "I'd never have told you Christie's secret, except that you're trying so hard to help him. You see—Christie wants more than anything else to be an artist himself. He's been studying and painting—trying to learn as much as he could before he went away to school. But when he found out that his mother was too sick to go on working, he knew he'd have to stay home and work to take care of her—and give up the scholarship—" Miss McDonell sighed.

"You can imagine how hard it was for the boy,"

she went on. "But he was determined not to let his mother know how much he was giving up. So —he told me he was going to hide all his paints and his paintings, to make her think he had forgotten about them. Those were Christie's paintings you saw on the island—"

"And it must have been Christie's paints we saw in the boat that day," Pip exclaimed. "We were afraid he was *smuggling* when we saw him come home from the island in the middle of the night. Thank heavens he wasn't! But, oh dear, if the paintings aren't Jacques Touraine's, I'm afraid that's our last hope gone."

Miss McDonell looked thoughtful for a moment. "I'm still trying to remember where I've heard that name," she closed her eyes, then opened them wide. "I know!" she exclaimed, "I remember now. There's a box downstairs in the basement storeroom with that name on it! Goodness knows how long it's been there. I asked about it when I first came to the library, but even then no one remembered anything about it."

"Oh, could we see it?" the girls asked breath-lessly.

Miss McDonell hesitated, then she said, "I can't think of any reason why not. I'd like to have another look at it myself. Come along."

She led the way to the basement, and in a far corner they found a square packing box with a label tacked on top. Pip leaned down to blow the dust aside, and sneezed. Then she pointed to the neat printing.

"Please hold for Jacques Touraine," she read.

"Oh, it *is* Frenchy—" the girls exclaimed in excitement. "He must have left the box here, maybe with some message inside. Let's open it and see."

But Miss McDonell was firm. "If Christie and his mother are Frenchy's relatives, they're the only ones who have a right to touch this box. Only—" she paused and frowned, "Christie's mother is ill—"

"And suppose Christie won't come?" Molly-O wrung her hands.

"I'll talk to Uncle Toby," Miss McDonell said. "*He'll* get Christie here."

"Daddy will be home for dinner," Molly added. "He's so interested in Christie, maybe he'll come too."

They met that evening in the Holland Library basement.

It was Uncle Toby who hammered the chisel and pried up the top of the wooden crate. The others stood in a solemn circle. As the rusty nails made a screechy sound, Molly-O touched Pip's hand. "I can hardly bear this," she whispered.

The next moment their faces fell in disappointment.

The box was filled with books, closely packed. When Uncle Toby lifted the first row, then the

second, and the third, there were only more books
—clear down to the bottom.

"Well," Uncle Toby said, "I suppose Frenchy

left his books in the library here because he was afraid the dampness on the island would ruin them. But I'm afraid there's nothing of any value." He turned to Christie. "I'm sorry, lad."

Christie only nodded. His face showed no expression, except that his mouth twitched a bit at the corners, with a disappointment he couldn't hide.

Just as Uncle Toby put the last books back in the box, Pip started forward. She saw something that made her catch her breath. Molly-O saw it at the same moment and they both pointed. "Wait! *Look at that book—*"

The others leaned forward curiously. The book was an old one, like the others, bound in a drab, brown cover. *Principles of Architecture* was the title—the author's name was *J. M. Chateau.* The girls were pointing at something green that had fallen out between the pages.

"What's that?" Molly and Pip asked in one breath. "It looks like *money!*"

Uncle Toby turned the book upside down and a whole shower of twenty—thirty—even fifty-dollar bills tumbled out.

They were all speechless for a minute.

"This must have been all of Frenchy's savings," Mr. Moore said finally. "That's what his note meant. He hid the money here because so many people were afraid of putting money in banks in those days. Frenchy intended, I'm sure, to come back and get the money after his trip home. But I wonder how he could have saved so much." He looked at the stack of banknotes.

"I can answer that," Uncle Toby said. "Frenchy never spent a penny on himself, except the little he needed to live. His big dream was to study to be an artist and he'd saved everything toward that time."

"Only that time never came," Miss McDonell said softly. "At least for Frenchy. But now, perhaps Christie can carry out his great-uncle's dream and study art—"

They all turned to look at the boy.

"There's enough money here," Uncle Toby told Christie, "to take care of your mother for a year. So you can take your scholarship!"

"Remember what Frenchy's note said," Pip exclaimed suddenly. "He said, 'Everything left in *Chateau*'—and we thought he meant the castle, in French!"

"But he really meant the book, by *Chateau*," Molly finished. "Poor Frenchy," she sighed. "I'm so sorry he had to die before he got his wish. Now maybe Christie can try to get it for him."

The last week of vacation was the happiest of all.

First came the news that Christie's great-uncle

had left enough savings to take care of Christie's mother, so the boy could take his scholarship.

"After that," Mrs. Anderson said, "the doctors promise that I'll be able to work again."

The change in Christie, almost overnight, was wonderful to see. His blue eyes were as serious as ever, but the worry was gone from them, and his laugh had a new, carefree sound.

"Christie's mother seems like a new person, too," Mrs. Moore told the girls when she came home from a call at Mrs. Anderson's. "She's sitting up, feeling stronger every day. When I promised to bring over some fried chicken and biscuits tomorrow, she looked positively *hungry*."

There was plenty of time to visit Uncle Toby. Mrs. Moore came too. She promised to exchange a special African violet for one of Mrs. Tobert's own plants.

On the last afternoon the girls had two surprises. First, Christie offered to take them out to the castle in his boat for a final visit. He even went into the castle with them, and helped them find the nail that Uncle Toby had left half-driven in the corner of the dining room floor.

"Isn't it wonderful!" Molly said privately, to Pip. "Christie doesn't feel a bit badly about coming to the castle any more!"

The second surprise came from Clementina. "What do you think she's done?" Uncle Toby beamed when the girls went the last afternoon to say good-bye. "Clementina's gone and had three kittens!"

"I thought you said Clementina had run down," Molly said reproachfully.

"Well, she's *running* down—but she hasn't stopped yet," Uncle Toby chuckled. "Just as well, too. There's a kitten for us to keep—just to remind Mother and me—and Clementina—that we need something young in the house. And there's one for each of you girls. Mr. Moore says he'll be back on Seaway business next month—and that'll be about time to take them home. Maybe they'll remind you of your vacation at Alexandria Bay."

"I'll name mine Alex for Alexandria Bay," Molly said.

"And I'll call mine Toby after Uncle Toby," Pip added promptly.

"Oh, they're darling!" the girls exclaimed together as they leaned over the box where Clementina displayed her babies proudly. "They'll always make us think of the wonderful time we've had here."

Driving away very early next morning, the girls looked through the back window of the station wagon for a final glimpse of their cottage, and the castle towers. A gray mist hung over the river, just as it had on the first evening they arrived, and only the tops of the castle turrets rose out of the silver fog. Sunken Rock Lighthouse sent its beams faithfully through the pearly light, round and round, round and round.

"Do you remember how mysterious the castle looked when we first saw it?" Molly asked. "We thought we must have dreamed it. But we found the answer to its secret."

They drove a way in silence, then Mrs. Moore said thoughtfully, "Perhaps there still is a secret. I think each one of us has a secret castle—the thing we dream of and want most in all the world. And we each have a different one."

"Christie's found *his* secret castle," Molly-O said. "Maybe someday we'll find ours."

Pip looked out of the window at a green field sloping down to the river. "Just think—" she drew a long breath. "This time tomorrow we'll be riding Treasure again. It's funny—" she frowned, "I haven't been one bit homesick until this minute. Now I can hardly wait to see Mommy and Daddy and Treasure. Even Jim and Bim," she added generously.

"I guess the nicest part of vacation is going home," Molly-O said, "especially when we can stop and get ice cream cones on the way." She patted her tummy thoughtfully. "I don't know how it could have happened so soon after breakfast, but I'm *hungry*."

About the Author

ANNE COLVER lives in Irvington-on-Hudson, has two children and the usual entanglements of suburban living: car pools, P.T.A., a Sheltie dog, etc. There's also Ebony, the horse, owned jointly by the author's daughter Kate and her best friend Ellen.

ANNE COLVER has been writing for many years and her previously published books for young people include, *Yankee Doodle Painter, Old Bet,* and *Borrowed Treasure* (another Molly-O and Pip story).

A NOTE ON THE TYPE
IN WHICH THIS BOOK IS SET

The text of this book is set in Caledonia, a Linotype face designed by W. A. Dwiggins. This type belongs to the family of printing types called "modern face" by printers—a term used to mark the change in style of type-letters that occurred about 1800. Caledonia borders on the general design of Scotch Modern, but is more freely drawn than that letter.

The book was composed, printed, and bound by H. Wolff, New York, typography by Tere LoPrete.